DARK EDGE

Other Books in The COIL Series

Dark Liaison, Book One
Dark Hearted, Book Two
Dark Rule, Book Three
Dark Vessel, Book Four
Dark Zeal, Book Five

Books in The COIL Legacy Series

Distant Boundary, Prequel
Distant Contact, Book One
Distant Front, Book Two
Distant Harm, Book Three

Other Books by D.I. Telbat

Arabian Variable
Called To Gobi
COIL Extractions: Short Story Collection
COIL Recruits: Short Story Collection
God's Colonel
Soldier of Hope
Leeward Set: Fury in the Storm, *Book One*
Leeward Set: Tears in the Wind, Book Two
The Legend of Okeanos
The Steadfast Series: America's Last Days

Coming Soon
Last Dawn Trilogy

DARK EDGE
A CHRISTIAN SUSPENSE NOVELLA

Prequel to The COIL Series

D.I. Telbat

In Season Publications
USA

Copyright © 2015 by D.I. Telbat

All rights reserved. No part of this publication may be reproduced, distributed or transmitted in any form or by any means, including photocopying, recording, or other electronic or mechanical methods, without the prior written permission of the publisher, except in the case of brief quotations embodied in critical reviews and certain other noncommercial uses permitted by copyright law. For permission requests, write to the publisher, In Season Publications at https://ditelbat.com/contact/.

Publisher's Note: This is a work of fiction. Names, characters, places, and incidents are a product of the author's imagination. Locales and public names are sometimes used for atmospheric purposes. Any resemblance to actual people, living or dead, or to businesses, companies, events, institutions, or locales is completely coincidental.

Printed in the United States of America

Dark Edge: Prequel to the COIL Series/D.I. Telbat
1st ed., updated 11/2018
Christian Suspense

ISBN 978-0-9862372-0-1

Book Layout ©2013 BookDesignTemplates.com
Cover Design by Streetlight Graphics

To those whom Christ has won,
To those who win others for Christ.

CHAPTER ONE

The Mole

Corban Dowler stopped his Ducati Diavel motorcycle on the bridge south of London's Buckingham Palace. He hastily stripped off his leather gloves and pitched them into the water below. His fake nose peeled off with more difficulty, followed by the cheekbone plaster. His cap along with the rest of his disguise disappeared over the rail.

Revving the throttle, he looked back toward King's Road. The street was quiet now just after midnight, but they were certain to be scrambling to track his whereabouts. A veteran CIA agent didn't disobey a kill order without causing panic up the hierarchy of powerful men who could rain down legions of hit men upon him.

Crossing the river, Corban raced his 162-

horsepower beast toward Shard London Bridge, doubling back on any pursuers. If they spotted him, he could out-maneuver them on his motorcycle, but he wanted to see them first.

Who would the Agency send to kill him? No doubt the CIA would sanction another MI6 resource to take Corban out, since he'd failed to assassinate a treasonous MI6 agent.

Below Shard London Bridge, Corban parked the Italian-made bike and climbed into a parked black Escalade. He drove toward St. Paul's Cathedral, his eyes peeled for a hunter-tracer team.

Finally finished with killing for his government, Corban felt the weight of that decision lifted from his shoulders. Kenneth Whitlock had been a low-level embarrassment to the SIS, Britain's intelligence sector, but the man's loyalties to North Korea were hardly worth killing him for. Whitlock was in love with a Korean diplomat—probably a spy herself. No one knew how long Whitlock had been seeing the woman, but he'd had no access to intel to pass on that would compromise England, anyway.

Even if Whitlock had been a higher level mole in the program, Corban still wouldn't have killed him. Sure, he'd never disobeyed a kill order before, but he'd never before believed in the Savior who had died for him, either. Deputy Director William

"Chip" Buchanen hadn't taken Corban seriously that fall when he'd told him he didn't want to kill any longer—traitors or otherwise. No more spy hunting, Corban had stated.

Now came the tricky part, the risky stage of his plan. His refusal to kill Whitlock meant the end of Corban's government career in the least, but it probably meant the end of his life as well. Unless he could implement his plan on time.

He parked on Oxford Street and retrieved a gray wig and thick glasses from the glove box. The disguise would get him through airport security. London's camera system could watch him throughout the city, but no one would be checking that footage for an hour or two. Even when they did begin to follow his escape route, he wasn't about to make it easy on them. He could learn to serve Jesus Christ in the new birth he'd been given, but only if he survived the next twenty-four hours.

First, he expected a CIA hunter-tracer team to be dispatched to catch or kill him. He knew they'd do this, utilizing any allied country's assets, because Corban had been a mole-hunter half his life. Though he wasn't a mole or a traitor, his failure to kill Whitlock would flag him as a threat. And threats were often annihilated before intel could be compromised. The report would be sealed, his body never found, and the risk would be neutralized.

Besides the team, a lone operator would also be given an independent kill order with Corban's name on it, someone he probably knew, but deadly, nonetheless. The assassin would be a specialist of the highest caliber, maybe even an agent he'd trained himself. The CIA wasn't above using anyone local to silence a threat—whether American, British, French, German, or Chinese.

Corban checked his special operations watch. Almost two hours had passed since he'd left Whitlock alive. He'd give them five more minutes to get into place, then he'd make the call to his wife, Janice.

He surveyed his mirrors constantly—a newspaper truck passed with an early morning delivery, a car with thumping music coasted by, a little rain sprinkled on the windshield. Nothing went unnoticed as long as he was being hunted.

The phone he took from the glove box had never been used. He dialed his home in New York City where it was early evening. It rang five times before Janice picked up.

"I just wanted to tell you it's over, Janice." Corban grit his teeth, hating the very words he had to say, even though it was all meant to protect her. "We're done. Things have been rockier much longer than I've been willing to admit."

There was silence for a moment. He could hear her breath shudder over the long distance.

"Corban, you're a Christian now." Her voice cracked. Though she was a take-charge woman, Janice was sensitive to harsh words. "Is this because I found out about your career? You have to give these things time."

"We've given it enough time, Janice. It's like our walk in the park last week. No, don't say anything! We couldn't even be ourselves. I've ruined our marriage with my deceit. I won't bother you any longer."

"Corban, I don't—"

"Listen to me!"

"What?"

"Goodbye."

He hung up and stared at the phone. Tears blurred his vision, and he knew the new heart of compassion God had given him was taking affect. The conversation had gone exactly as he'd planned, every word perfectly quoted from a script in his mind. All international calls to the US were recorded, but it would take anywhere between an hour and a day to recover that specific call. At that point, the CIA would know Corban was apparently done with his wife, and not just his country. She couldn't be used against him if they thought she meant nothing to him. All ties had been cut.

But Janice did mean something to him. Only recently she'd discovered what he did for a living. Between his own faith in God's direction and Janice's urgings, Corban had realized he couldn't continue serving his country as a killer any longer.

Their marriage had been on the edge for years—thanks to Corban never being home, his life obsessed with foreign matters, and his dark moods.

The most recent problem had been his inability to reveal to her his plan to leave the CIA permanently. She had to believe his leaving her was real in order to convince any investigators that it was real. Except, he'd left her a breadcrumb for later: they hadn't walked in the park last week. They'd never walked in the park. It was too dangerous in his line of work. That false statement alone would signal to her that he wasn't in a normal state of mind.

"Keep her safe, Lord. She's in Your hands."

Corban checked his mirrors, looked up at the camera posts over the sidewalk, and exited the car. He walked in view of a dozen cameras for ten minutes, then hailed a taxi. The trail was intentional, until he wanted to leave no trail at all. In the taxi, he shed his disguise and applied a fake beard as the taxi approached the airport.

Inside the terminal, he purchased a new cell phone and checked messages on a bulletin board system left over from his Cold War days. Everything was in place. He was going to India.

CHAPTER TWO

The Sanction

"You deal with this muddle, Chip!" CIA Director Jacob Dench shouted in his sterile Langley office. "Corban Dowler is your mess. Clean it up!"

"Jake, it's not that simple." Deputy Director William "Chip" Buchanen crossed his legs while he sat in front of Dench's broad mahogany desk. He wondered why such a powerful man had such uncomfortable chairs for his guests. But then he realized he already knew the answer: Dench liked to watch people squirm in discomfort, as well as under his intimidation. "We're talking about Corban here, not some newbie. He knows every trick in the book because he wrote the book. Whatever move you and I respond with here—it'll be one he already knows. We have protocols. Corban will write new ones for himself."

"Yeah, but you suspected he'd changed. That's why we tested him with that London contract in the first place. What was the mole's name?"

"Kenneth Whitlock. A nobody."

"Right. You already knew Corban had lost his edge. Now it's been confirmed. So you're the one to get him, or find someone who can. Where are your loyalties, Chip?"

Chip bowed his head and tried to think strategically. Corban was his friend, or had been, but refusing to kill Whitlock potentially changed everything. The warrant for Corban's death had been signed and a body disposal team was probably on standby.

"I suggest we recall him, Jake, but first recall the H-T team we already dispatched. He'll know we sent hunter-tracers after him."

"Like you said: it's protocol. Let's keep up appearances until we can figure out his play." The director shrugged. "Why recall the team? A traitor is on the run. We know he's a traitor because he's running. You were right to have observers on Whitlock to see if Corban would falter. Maybe Corban's loyalties are with the North Koreans, too."

"That's not the problem. I told you, he has new

religious convictions. I say we recall him and re-task him to another branch, something without wet work. He doesn't want to be sanctioned for those types of jobs anymore."

"How can we re-task a man we can't trust?" Dench slammed his fist on his desktop calendar. "No, you take him out, Chip! Do it as quietly as you can, before Corban can set up his defenses. We don't want a defector on our hands."

"And that brings up some risk calculations our boys did." Chip sighed. "If Corban turns on us—"

"He's already turned!"

"I mean, if Corban responds aggressively with an actual offensive because of our pursuit of him, he could literally dismantle the Agency."

"No single man is that powerful. We have safeguards."

"Maybe intelligence safeguards, but what about the Endgame Protocol?"

"It's a myth, Chip. A story to make newbie agents dream. There's no such thing as an Endgame Protocol. We'd know it if Corban or anyone else had a network of spy contacts powerful enough to take us on—or to defend him from the full wrath of the United States government."

"But this is Corban Dowler." Chip chuckled and rubbed his jaw, wishing he was sitting in the director's chair giving Dench orders. "He's been in the shadows for thirty years. Who are we to say he doesn't have resources off the grid? After all, he did design our misinformation database."

Dench rose from his chair and walked around his desk, his eyes never leaving Chip's face. Chip flinched when the director reached toward him. Though Chip was in better shape than Dench, he still didn't want to grapple with his superior in his own office.

Instead, Dench plucked the files from under Chip's arm, then sat on the edge of his desk.

"I assume you brought these for some reason." The man scanned through the six files. "Consider me advised otherwise, but I'm sanctioning Corban's end. I'm hardly in the mood for arguing, Chip, but I do trust you. After all, I'm trusting you with my daughter's search, aren't I? Any word on Kimberly?"

"Nothing conclusive. I'm sorry."

"What are the rumors, then? We have people in India. They have to know something! Two weeks without contact, Chip. This is my daughter we're talking about!"

"Rumors. Your daughter was helping low-caste people in Haridwar on the Ganges River. You know her work was making enemies. Sharing freedom in Jesus to *Dalits* isn't popular."

"So, is she dead or alive, Chip? Come on!"

"Kidnapped, it seems. If they'd dumped her body, it would've surfaced by now since she's a Westerner."

Dench shook his head.

"Sharing Jesus. My own daughter." He cursed. "I swear, she and Corban are plotting against me! Corban finds religion and my own daughter can't stop spreading it."

"This is our top priority in India, Jake. I'll let you know the minute we have any hard facts. Our best Far East agents are on it."

"Alright. Let's get back to Corban." Dench tossed five files onto his desk, but kept the sixth one. "You've classified the guy in this file higher than the others. Why? Who's Nace Scanlon?"

"An MI6 spook, practically off the books." Chip smiled. If he was going after Corban, so be it. He would enjoy the chase. "If anyone can catch Corban, Nace Scanlon can. His codename is Pyvox. Corban knows we're coming after him, so we'll send something he can't see coming: poison."

"Poison? How's that?"

"Scanlon was a biochemist before he was trained at Britain's Fort Monckton. They say this creep has shatter-proof vials of sodium pentothal and halothane up his sleeves. He designed a formula for dieldrin and released it to the Asian black market. The pesticide can be absorbed through the skin, simple contact, and thirty minutes later, after a violent seizure—death."

"Yeah, but does Corban know him? This . . . Scanlon?"

"Not as far as we can tell. He might know of him, but Scanlon is an expert at disguises as well. He's trained at subterfuge, and he can track a bit-stream through a binary blizzard, or however they track people on the Internet nowadays."

"Who cares?" Dench laughed. "Let the techies do their thing, as long as we get Corban. Okay, send Scanlon after him. The Brits won't mind us using one of their own, seeing as we didn't take care of their Whitlock problem. They enjoy cleaning up our messes. Makes them feel superior."

"I'll get a message off to them."

"And Chip? Get another unrelated European team on this right away, too, besides the H-T team we already dispatched. Corban might expect one frontal assault, but I want a layered pursuit. I want Corban Dowler taken care of within the week!"

CHAPTER THREE

The Agent

Corban Dowler didn't like living on the run, but after a lifetime of clandestine reporting and shadowing active provocateurs, he'd learned to tolerate the lack of sleep and hasty meals. Though he was in enough danger to warrant hiding underground, he knew God wanted him to live up to his potential. The sheer magnitude of his resources were beyond the Agency's control or knowledge, so he was determined to take on the organization rather than disappear in silence.

Though Langley had shut down his personal digital access, he had a dozen other identities he'd used for various missions, and most of those had been black operations, now buried in sealed documents, hidden in numbered boxes, stored in a basement long forgotten. But the identities were still intact in his memory.

Most of his identities were completely fictional, but a couple had full livelihoods and reputations—because they'd been actual people at some point. Once caught or killed, terrorists or international enemies of the state often left behind estates and accounts that many foreign governments dared not claim for fear of reprisal. Corban had anticipated future hardships, so he'd claimed some of these covers as his own. Now that he had only himself to depend on, he still had what he'd built while he was a spy and a spy hunter. It was part of his Endgame Protocol—an agent's contingency plan if his own government turned against him.

In Paris, en route to India, Corban used a laptop to log into a Japanese proxy server, then tapped into a Langley database in San Diego. He couldn't identify who'd been activated against him, but high level assets had been mobilized, locked behind codenames recently implemented. The secrecy alone told him it was a major operation, maybe involving Director Jacob Dench himself. They were coming to kill him, and he could count on the very best the CIA and its allies could muster to prove their patriotism by shedding his blood.

Or worse, Corban had many international

enemies who would love to kill him, if they knew he was fair game and no longer under the shield of the CIA. But no, Corban decided. The CIA wouldn't risk him being captured by an aggressor from an enemy nation. The Agency would make sure he was killed, and quickly, to put him in the grave with all his secrets.

His watch beeped and he looked up. He saw an attractive Israeli woman across the terminal—beautiful, certainly, but he also knew her to be deadly. And she was right on time, her flight to Tel Aviv leaving minutes after his own to Bangalore.

Collecting his laptop and carry-on bag, he crossed the corridor and sat in a seat facing her own. Passing through Paris on his way to India had been intentional. Meeting the pretty Mossad agent was a top priority for his future work for Jesus Christ.

"May I ask you a question?" He spoke English, though having read her profile, he knew she also spoke German, Hebrew, and Arabic.

Her gaze was intense, as if she was able to see through the fake eyebrows and the plaster around his phony nose. He'd also applied makeup under his eyes and on his cheeks to give him a dark, gaunt appearance.

She browsed the corridor, maybe anticipating an

ambush. Only an experienced field agent was that cautious.

"I'm alone, Chloe." He crossed his legs and put his arm across the back of the chair next to him. "I come on behalf of my employer, Corban Dowler."

"Corban . . . Dowler?" Chloe Azmaveth frowned, and swiped the dark curls from her temple, perhaps to improve her peripheral vision. "Dowler's in no position to employ anyone, last I heard, which was pretty recent. What's your question?"

"Well, it's more of a proposition, actually. Dowler is being hunted because he became a Christian and refused to kill a man—a British traitor to the North Koreans."

"Dowler's a Christian?" She scoffed. "We must not be talking about the same Dowler! The Dowler I know . . . well, let's just say I'd prefer walking into the same room as a suicide bomber than be in the same room with him."

"In a few days, the Agency will allow Dowler to retire in peace. Then he wants to use his network to set up a Christian spy agency."

"The CIA will never allow Dowler to retire, unless it's to an unmarked grave." Chloe unbuttoned her blazer, as if she expected physical conflict. "Dowler's been around too long. He knows too much."

"That's precisely why they'll soon realize they're better off keeping him alive. They'll have to. Dowler has an Endgame Protocol."

"Figures. If anyone did, he would." She sat up a little straighter. "So, you said a Christian spy agency? How's that supposed to work?"

Corban hesitated as he noticed a large black man veer away from his approach when Corban looked his way. The man had a scar across the bridge of his nose and seemed familiar. But an airport identification on his belt marked him as a baggage administrator. Looking back at the Israeli agent, Corban noticed Chloe was now holding a pair of glasses. He knew she didn't wear glasses. She'd weaponized a pair of reading glasses, he guessed.

"Christians are dying for the gospel all over the world," Corban said. "Those of us who are Christians, like Dowler now, are so busy operating for amoral governments, we have no time to tend to God's people. But we could. Dowler wants you to help."

"Like I said, I don't want to be anywhere near Dowler. The man's a walking target—not to mention more dangerous than anyone I've heard about. You sound like you're an America, so you know how the top gunslinger in your Western movies attracts the most bullets."

"What's a few bullets if you could save souls?" Corban rose to his feet, and saw her tense. "Dowler will come for you in a few weeks."

"Well, I'm not going with him!" She laughed. "We've never even met!"

"I know you're a Christian, Chloe. Last October, you filed a DAR from Sydney stating that as a Christian, you were morally obligated to help persecuted Christians in Indonesia. Then you flew to Sumatra against your government's orders, and you saved lives."

"How . . . do you know about that? Daily activity reports are top secret." She stood up, the glasses gripped firmly in her fist. "Leaving the Mossad won't be any easier for me than Dowler leaving the Agency."

"Easy or not, we have to trust God with the details as we obey His call. Will you risk your life for God's people?"

"I—" She smiled and pocketed the glasses. "I've risked my life for my amoral country, as you called it. Seems as a Christian, I should gladly do the same for God's own people. You could say . . . I'm interested."

"All right, I'll tell Dowler you're in." Corban shifted his feet. "Tell me: is the black man over my right shoulder watching us?"

"Yes. A friend of yours?" The glasses came smoothly from her pocket again. "I've seen him before, in the Ukraine."

"Who does he belong to?"

"He's a Brit, I think. A Russian diplomat died in Moldova while he was there."

Corban turned as his flight number was called.

"That's my flight. Stay safe, Chloe. We'll be in touch."

"Wait. What about the Brit? You want me to, I don't know . . . distract him?"

"No, he already found me." Corban smiled. "Maybe I can turn him, huh? Preferably before he kills me."

Corban studied the faces of those in the airport terminal. His life depended on remembering their faces. If they were agents sent to kill him, he wanted to recognize them again if they approached him later.

"Sounds like something only Corban Dowler would be confident enough to say." She held out her hand. "Go with God, sir. It's an honor to hear you're finally in the shadow of the cross."

Corban shook her hand then left to board his flight. The last he saw, the black agent—probably an assassin—was approaching Chloe Azmaveth at her departure gate. But Corban didn't worry about her.

If she was half as skilled as her IDF profile claimed she was, the British assassin would have his hands full.

CHAPTER FOUR

The Poison

As Nace "Pyvox" Scanlon passed his target, he skillfully brushed the back of the man's hand. Within an hour, the man would be dead. Maybe then the other agents trying to catch Corban Dowler would get out of his way and let him work.

In the men's restroom, Scanlon took off his glove and flushed it down the toilet, the poison with it. No one would ever know he'd just killed a German agent in the Paris airport deli, but death was part of being a government specialist. They should've been more careful approaching such a highly valued mark as Corban Dowler.

Scanlon paused at the sink and washed his hands as he scowled at himself in the mirror. At fifty-two, he looked about sixty, maybe older with the scar across his nose. The hard life of an assassin had worn away the years faster than he'd been able to enjoy them. In fact, he'd not truly enjoyed any of those years. As a chemist, he'd slaved in the lab without taking vacations or making friends. There were no trophies on his shelf at home to celebrate his years of sacrifice for the government that barely acknowledged him.

And he now hunted a man much like himself. Well, nearly. Scanlon was fascinated with Corban Dowler. He'd heard of the man over the years—a lone operator, a ghost from Langley who could infiltrate any nation and access any target that needed to be eliminated. Was he good enough to take out Corban?

"*Aconitum napellus*," Scanlon said to the mirror. The name had a nice sound to it—a deadly and almost romantic ring. Any part of the monkshood plant was deadly, inducing heart failure. It was the poison he'd chosen with which to kill Corban. No one would ever know.

However, his job had become quite difficult. German agents in the airport had about captured Corban, but Scanlon's orders were to kill him. In the process of getting to his target before the Germans, Scanlon knew Corban had made him.

And then there was the Israeli woman, Chloe

Azmaveth. He'd run her face in his portable recognition software as soon as he'd seen Corban talking to her. She was connected to the Mossad, a mid-level agent heading home after an operation in Argentina. Scanlon had approached her after Corban boarded his jet to India. When he was just a dozen paces from her, she'd turned, a pair of reading glasses in her hand. She'd smiled and shook her head at him, her confidence suggesting she was more than a mid-level agent, even if that was all her file said.

So instead of questioning and killing Chloe Azmaveth, Scanlon had swiped the German operator's hand. Eventually, they might suspect it was his doing, but no one would bother trying to prove it, he hoped. It was more blood on the Americans' hands for hiring a crowd of assassins when one precision instrument as himself was required for someone of Corban Dowler's caliber.

Leaving the restroom, Scanlon found the nearest ticket booth and purchased a flight for Bangalore. India was a likely place for a fugitive to hide—in the midst of a billion people. But Scanlon knew Corban wasn't a man to hide from anyone. He had a feeling of foreboding that Corban was drawing him in. After all, Corban had made him in the airport, yet he had calmly boarded his plane anyway.

But Scanlon was determined to see Corban die in India. Then he'd return to the Thames to await another ring on his phone with the next promising contract. In a week, he would forget the face of Corban Dowler. Scanlon never remembered the dead.

CHAPTER FIVE

The Lie

CIA Director Jacob Dench sipped his vodka, then set the glass down and cracked open his shotgun. It was a double barrel .12 gauge. Divorced and alone on his estate in East Maryland, he saw no reason why he shouldn't have a hobby involving guns. And Russian vodka.

After reloading the shotgun, he threw the vodka glass into the night sky. His balcony provided the perfect shooting platform. The shotgun butt found its home against his shoulder and he pulled the trigger. The blast echoed across the manmade lake, around which only four mansions had been built. If the residents didn't like his late night hobby, they'd never said anything.

"Because they know who I am," Dench said into

the darkness. He poured himself another shot in a new glass and reloaded the gun.

It had been a particularly bad day, and that usually meant his hobby lasted a little later than usual. Sure, drinking vodka was probably un-American, especially for an intelligence administrator who'd earned his merits during the Cold War fighting Russians in East Germany. But it didn't matter any more. Though he was a patriot, it seemed like it had all been for naught. Communism was still threatening the world, and Russia was still flexing her muscles against weaker nations.

And then there was Corban Dowler. If Dench had made a bet thirty years earlier, he would've wagered that Dowler would die before he ever turned against the Agency, America, and his family. But he had turned. And for what? His God? A self-proclaimed Savior from two millennia ago?

Dench swore as he remembered his own daughter was a Christian. Her faith had been her downfall as well. That was her mother's doing, sometime after the divorce. Now Kim was gone—kidnapped and probably sold into some human trafficking slum-ring in India. It was nearly impossible to trace such transactions, and more impossible to care much for a girl he'd never taken the time to know.

"*Christians.*" Dench cursed, and threw another glass into the sky. When he shot it, the glass exploded. He flinched away but it was too late. The shotgun clattered onto the deck as he held his cheek, blood dribbling past a piece of embedded glass.

He plucked out the glass, causing the wound to leak freely, but he didn't care. All that mattered was winning, and right now, because of Corban Dowler, he was losing.

A report from Paris had arrived through Chip. A German agent had been mysteriously murdered, probably poisoned, in Paris. That meant Nace "Pyvox" Scanlon was on Dowler's trail, but there was still no sign of either man—the hunter or the hunted.

As long as Dowler was alive, he was a threat to Dench's legacy. Dowler had to die. The best the Agency had to offer, even though hardly anyone knew he existed, had refused to kill his target. Sure, it happened with agents, but not seasoned hunter-tracer agents who had nearly two-hundred operations under his belt. And those were just the ones in his file.

Dench frowned at the piece of glass he'd taken from his cheek. The deck light passed through it, bent the light, and caused a tiny prism.

Bending. Yes, Dench thought. That was the answer to Paris and the dead German. The problem that Dowler had become simply needed to be bent to Dench's satisfaction. Even Dowler himself would appreciate it, wouldn't he?

Pocketing the piece of glass as a memento of the moment, Dench entered the house and went to his study. He logged into his work server via an encrypted satellite signal, and studied the Paris report more carefully. His deceit settled into place.

If Dowler simply refused to kill anymore, that was a quiet problem for the Agency. But if he could turn Dowler into the Paris killer—and sell it to the Germans—then Dowler would be a problem for all of America. The President himself would send resources overseas to take care of Dowler. In the end, everyone would praise him, Jacob Dench, for how he'd handled the Corban Dowler problem.

So, Dowler didn't want to kill America's enemies? Then Dowler would become America's enemy number one—a hated murderer, a coward who poisoned random people in airports.

Dench touched his cheek and admired the blood on his fingertips. No stitches. He wanted to remember this night through the remnant scar as the night he finalized Corban Dowler's demise!

CHAPTER SIX

The Problem

"You must bathe in the river, my friend. The positive energy could give you luck for the rest of your life."

Corban acted as if he was considering the *Mumbaikar's* words about bathing in India's Ganges River, but he had other things on his mind. Besides, he didn't believe in luck or positive energy from dirty water. The Hindu man moved on through the crowd—one man in a throng of millions—but Corban remained on the edge of the river.

He'd arrived in Haridwar in northern India during the *Kumbh Mela* pilgrimage, the world's largest religious festival. Hindu believers stripped down to their underclothes and walked into the cold water. It was to be done before dawn, but now, two hours after dawn, the shoreline was indistinguishable through the brown bodies and excited visitors. On the sloped bank where Corban stood, he could see several hundred thousand people pressing shoulder to shoulder in or out of the filthy water, which swirled around temple towers, their very foundations built on the bed of the river.

"You need to be high on *Vishnu* and *gonja* to get in that water," an Australian man's voice said. Corban turned to see a middle-aged man wearing a long-sleeved *kurta*. He'd arrived in a rickshaw, the runner panting heavily nearby. "I came as you asked."

Corban didn't offer his hand. He wasn't sure if the press of bodies was actually dangerous or if they served as a safety net. Whoever was hunting him could already be in the city—maybe even posing as one of the local snake charmers, vendors, or Hindu *gewgaws* who worked the crowd.

"Where's the girl?" While Corban continued to keep watch for an enemy, he glanced at the Australian agent, an ASIS specialist. Alan Doutrice wasn't an enemy, but he wasn't necessarily a friend, either. The man was more loyal to money than to country, and his connections to the underworld of India had been called upon more than a few times by Corban through the years. "One phone call, and the money is transferred."

"It won't help you even if you do know where the girl is." Alan stepped out of the rickshaw. The rickshaw owner plodded off, squeezing through a wave of hermits who'd apparently sworn off wearing clothing in exchange for wearing wreaths and garlands of marigolds. "I feel almost guilty for taking your money. *Almost.* The girl is safer than the gold in your Fort Knox."

"A kidnapped American is hardly safe here!" Corban said through clenched teeth. "Just tell me what I need to know."

"The girl is held in there—see the gray tower? The *Sadhus* holds court from there. His followers are countless. There are one hundred million Hindus attending *Kumbh Mela* in four cities in the next fifty-five days. She'll be impossible to recover."

Using the height that the slope gave him to see over the throng, Corban studied a thirty-foot tall round building, a walkway circling it six feet above the river surface. What looked like Christmas lights were strung in a tangle around its roof. The mass of humanity seemed to fill every inch of the water, but they gave wide berth to the tower.

He took in the details before he noticed three men in blazers on the walkway. Though their guns weren't visible, he was sure they were armed, concealing them under their jackets. It seemed they were bodyguards.

"Tell me about this *Sadhus* man."

"A *Sadhus* is a holy man, not a name. But this one is known as the *Sadhus*. He controls more worshippers in this region than any other *Sadhus*. With a word, he can muster one thousand Hindus, or even a million. That's why it's impossible to get the girl out. The police won't even touch the *Sadhus*."

"Let me worry about getting her out. It's just the three outside?" Corban didn't need to disguise his gaze. He was a face amongst a sea of faces. "How many inside?"

"At least five, usually, but I don't know for sure. You just called me two days ago. I don't know everything."

"You've told me enough." Corban looked away from the river. A Caucasian face caught his eye, then it was lost in the crowd. He recognized the face from the Paris airport. "You'd better leave. I've got it from here. If I need—"

But Alan Doutrice was already gone, apparently trusting Corban to make the payment as agreed. One last time, Corban measured the dimensions of the Hindu tower where the girl was being held, then moved up the bank past all the chatting and crying Indians.

He wasn't tall enough to see over all those around him, but if he could get high enough up the slope . . . As he weaved through the swarm of bodies, he took off his jacket and bent down to dip his hand into a puddle. Hoping it was mud, he dabbed some onto his face and into his hair. With his features sufficiently altered for the moment, he turned and climbed the cement stairs built into the slope until he could look down at the throng. It took mere seconds to spot the hunter-tracer team. They were light-skinned and fully clothed, so they stood out in the half-naked crowd of brown bodies. Two others looked familiar from Paris as well, but their attention was directed elsewhere. They had to be part of a hunter-tracer team, and that meant Corban's plans in India just became much more complicated.

Members of the H-T team were separately converging on a tall muscled black man, whom Corban guessed was over fifty. The tall man wore a tan suit without a tie, and carried a small bag, as if he'd recently arrived in town. He was definitely the baggage man from Paris, identified by the scar—a killer who apparently didn't realize he was about to be killed himself. The agents were moving like a pride of lions toward their prey. There was no question as to their intent towards the tall black man.

The man who Chloe had said was a Brit stood in the very place Corban had been just ten minutes earlier, next to another rickshaw. For a hunter-tracer team—or possibly two teams—to be on Corban's trail so soon, he surmised they were government-sponsored and not merely independent mercenary teams. Private assassins could be resourceful, but not as rapidly deployed as these.

At the moment, the agents seemed unaware of Corban's presence. Instead of remaining exposed on the elevated steps, he chose to lose himself in the press of bodies closer to the riverbank, even though it drew him nearer the agents. When he reached the river, he squeezed through the bathers until he found himself directly below the Brit from Paris. Now so close, when the black man looked at Corban, there was unmistakable recognition on his face. Seeing the man straight on, Corban memorized his face and features so he could identify him later in an Agency database—if the man even lived through the morning. And since Corban was just getting to know this man, it wouldn't do to see him killed. After all, Corban was in India to save a life, not to lead one to his death.

Corban turned his head and nodded toward the nearest agents approaching the black man. The man seemed to understand the signal. He glanced around at the near-ambush, then darted into the crowd and was instantly in the water up to his waist. Fascinated by the man's speed, Corban watched as the Brit abandoned his bag, then disappeared in the polluted water.

Now Corban was close to being noticed by the other agents. He crouched as they passed him, pursuing as a pack of wolves after the Brit in the water. In a moment, Corban was back on the stairs, about to vacate the river scene. Though he knew he should leave, Corban remained mesmerized on the set of steps, admiring the crafty Brit's escape from harm. In the same situation, it was exactly what Corban himself would've done, he thought.

Farther out in the river, people were parting mysteriously. The man was but a shadow beneath the surface, seen only from Corban's viewpoint, but not by the team on the bank who was still searching the crowd for the Brit. Before they spotted Corban as well, he slipped over the hilltop onto a busy street. As he moved into the city, he smiled. He was about to secure his future, and yet, he'd just given a killer a very difficult decision to make. Would the man return the gesture and stop hunting him?

When Corban reached his hotel, he checked out and walked to a backup site—a parked rental car amongst a row of commuter cars. From the driver's seat, he prayed for guidance. He was there to save Kimberly Dench's life, but suddenly he was inclined to save another as well: the man who was trying to kill him.

Setting his laptop in the passenger seat, he logged into a server in Mumbai and got to work. It was going to be a long night.

CHAPTER SEVEN

The Recruit

Nace "Pyvox" Scanlon barely dodged an overburdened bus of passengers that careened past him without slowing. He paused, looking for a place to hide, at least until darkness covered the Indian city. Though he'd left the Ganges River two hours earlier, his clothes were still wet and muddy from sweating and falling in various alleys as he was chased.

Normally, he would've turned to face his enemies, but the German hunter-tracer team was seeing red. They were skilled professionals and brutally efficient, like hounds that anticipated his escape routes. And they were closing in.

He regretted the carelessness with which he'd killed the German assassin in Paris. If he would've continued his hunt for Corban on his own, all the force of German's intelligence community wouldn't be descending on him now. The dead man's teammates would probably never rest until he was sinking in a Haridwar sewer pond.

Panting, Scanlon put his back against a rickety wall and tugged a throwing knife from his left triceps. At least one member of the German team was a knife expert. And the knives he used weren't the normal kind. They were some sort of composite plastic that could pass through a metal detector.

Scanlon tucked the blade into his belt and pulled up his shirt sleeve. He usually traveled with several vials of choice poisons, but while running for his life, he'd lost all but one vial of a lachrymator, tear gas in a bottle, meant for dispersing in a crowd rather than for a single target.

A spare passport was sewn into his pant leg, so he didn't necessarily need to return to his hotel room. But returning to the airport wasn't the answer, either. The Germans seemed to have about a dozen assets in the city now, and probably at least that many locals in their employment.

Traveling inland was the answer, Scanlon decided. He would travel farther upriver, and reassess once he could get resupplied. It was humiliating to fail—a first time for him—but he couldn't complete the mission with a squad of assassins on his trail. Corban Dowler would receive a reprieve for now—not because the man had warned him at the river, but because Scanlon was outmatched at the moment.

Pushing away from the wall, he found himself directly in the path of two German operators. They both wore a local cloth over their shoulders, perhaps in an attempt to blend in. But Scanlon hadn't had time to disguise himself since leaving the river. Between avoiding agents and dodging knives—obviously not too successfully—he'd left himself exposed.

In that split second, staring into the eyes of a blond man in glasses, Scanlon thought about how disgraceful it would be to die in the hands of these foot soldiers. However well-trained they were, that's what they were to him. He'd been an independent operator for years, almost exclusively for the British. His craft had become sophisticated with most of his chemicals untraceable. Even those he called friends feared him.

Backing away from the agents, he reached for his sleeve. The lachrymator needed a distribution system, like a can of compressed air, but maybe if he threw it on the pavement hard enough . . .

Two more agents rounded the corner and

stopped with drawn sidearms. Scanlon looked around him. There were no bystanders he could push in front of any oncoming bullets. A dead end loomed behind him with only sales booths on both sides. Though he accepted that he was about to die and enter the great beyond, he didn't like leaving a sanctioned hit unfinished. It wasn't the legacy he had in mind. Now, someone else would kill Dowler, the true master, and—

Corban Dowler walked slowly behind the four German agents, and for an instant, Scanlon thought Corban had joined the Germans to kill him. But then he saw Corban carried a crooked tree branch. In the hands of a common man, a stick meant very little. However, a three-foot stick in the hands of a hunter-tracer ghost could be a game-changing weapon.

When Corban struck, Scanlon flinched. All of Corban's force went into that first blow against one of the gunmen, instantly paralyzing the man's arm and causing the gun to clatter to the street.

Proving he wasn't at all at the end of his age of fitness, Corban spun and kicked. He thrust the stick at the next gunman. The other two with knives were upon Corban then, and Scanlon saw his opportunity. While Corban was whipping the stick at the German team, Scanlon picked up the dropped gun and held it on the fighting men.

Though outnumbered, Corban didn't appear to be overwhelmed. The Germans had been overconfident while targeting Scanlon, but Corban had caught them off-guard.

The men seemed to see Scanlon at the same instant that they noticed the gun trained on them. In his hesitation to fire, they abandoned their scuffle and fled the scene, taking their injured with them.

Breathless, Corban dropped his stick, and Scanlon aimed at his target's chest, content with taking a break from his preferred method of elimination just this once, if it meant a finished contract.

"Seems like the right way to repay the one who's now saved your life twice," Corban said, his head down and hands clenched into fists.

"I can't afford to get sentimental. You know who I am."

"Pyvox, right?" Corban raised his head and looked Scanlon in the face. "You're not that much of a mystery, Nace Scanlon. You're like the rest of us—lost in a sea of darkness, desperate and lonely, thinking there's no other path for you."

"It is indeed my path." Scanlon wasn't amused, or even bothered. All of his targets, given the chance, begged for mercy in their own ways. "It's the only path I know."

"No, it isn't. Come on. We have a girl to rescue. You want to still be standing there when the BND come back?"

"German's Federal Intelligence Service is in India to kill you." Scanlon chuckled, enjoying the banter with a peer, an equal of the highest caliber.

"Yeah, well, when they come back for me, who do you think they'll kill first—the man with the gun or the man with empty hands? Come on."

Scanlon's smile disappeared. This man he was tracking to kill was actually talking to him as if he were a partner!

"What's this business about a girl to save?" Scanlon felt his resolve soften. This had never happened before—almost as if something had turned off the savagery inside him. The only thing he could think to blame it on was his dip in the holy Ganges, and he knew that polluted water had no special powers. "I work alone. I'm not going anywhere with you."

"Fine." Corban held up his hand as if to signal his departure. "After I show you where she is, you can rescue her yourself—alone, as you wish."

Corban walked away. Scanlon looked to his left and right, then tossed the gun into a seller's booth.

"That's not what I meant. Hey!"

Scanlon cursed and stomped after Corban, yet kept a careful eye out for the Germans.

CHAPTER EIGHT

The Rescue

Corban Dowler sat in a borrowed motorboat two hundred yards upriver from the temple tower in which Kimberly Dench was being held. With more preparation and better resources, he would've had night vision and more backup, but as things stood, he was just glad the Germans hadn't found them again. As for backup, he had Nace "Pyvox" Scanlon, a man contracted to kill him.

This wasn't the first time Corban had appealed to an enemy's sense of honor to do the right thing against all odds. But this was the first time Corban had recruited an enemy for a purpose that wasn't expressly selfish. He'd invited Scanlon to join him first for Scanlon's sake, and second, to help him free Kimberly.

According to schedule, ten minutes had passed so Corban started the motor. In the distance, the Hindu temple tower was lit up by its sparkling lights, which illuminated several gunmen on the walkway above the water.

What the lights didn't illuminate, hidden in the shadows of the walkway, was Nace Scanlon in the water wearing a dark wetsuit.

Scanlon had bought a tank of compressed air and attached it to a four milligram vial of lachrymator. The powerful form of tear gas would burn the eyes, throat, and skin upon dispersion. Corban approved of the offensive method since it was a non-lethal weapon system. Scanlon's deadly poisons for which he was known had been lost, the man had claimed, but Corban didn't completely trust his word.

As Corban slowly motored the five-seat boat toward the tower, he appreciated the quiet water. In a few hours, millions of lost souls would begin to gather again for another day of *Kumbh Mela*.

Before he reached the tower, Corban adjusted the dark beard that covered his cheeks and chin. Thick-rimmed glasses completed the disguise he'd used many times. The personality was known in Muslim circles as an arms dealer and sometimes smuggler. But as well-known as his false identity was, Corban didn't like going into a meeting without some sort of defensive weapon on his person. If he survived this op, maybe he'd turn his glasses into a weapon like Chloe had done, perhaps with a tranquilizer dart. Even a single-fire weapon would be better than what he had now—nothing but his hand-to-hand skills against men with automatic weapons.

Two of the gunmen on the tower walkway leaned over the edge and caught the bow of the boat as Corban drifted up to them. They held the small vessel as he received one of their hands to pull him onto the walkway.

For just an instant, Corban thought he glimpsed Scanlon below the walkway, submerged up to his neck in the calm water. Corban prayed that Scanlon didn't have an ulterior motive for accompanying him on the rescue operation. He had to leave that in God's hands—to watch over what Corban couldn't watch himself: his back.

Corban held his arms out as one man frisked him. As agreed, he'd arrive with no firearms.

He was led around the walkway, and a narrow door opened for him. Without hesitating, Corban entered the tower, the small circular room lit by candles, mirrors on the walls giving the room an illusion of being larger than it was. Four more gunmen stood against the mirrors, two on the left, and two on the right of Corban. In the center, seated on the floor, was a veiled, bowed person under drab clothing. It had to be Kimberly. Near her, the *Sadhus,* whom Alan Doutrice had described, sat on a large cushion that looked to be from a sofa. The man wore a permanent scowl, which was disconcerting on a supposed holy man's face.

"Peace to you," Corban said with an Arabic accent, and offered a low sustained nod that the *Sadhus* was free to interpret as a bow. "I am Muhammad ibn Affal. I have come for the American vermin."

The *Sadhus,* who wore a gold-colored robe, gestured toward another cushion. Dressed in baggy pants and shirt bought at the carnival bazaar, Corban seated himself, but he remained poised. In an instant, he could rise and defend himself or Kimberly.

"Tell us, Muhammad, how you like India?" The *Sadhus* spoke slowly in heavily accented English.

"I am honored to be here during your holiest of festivals." Corban spoke just as slowly, knowing he was being tested. Due to Pakistan's war in the north with India, Hindus and Muslims didn't usually ally themselves for extremist motives. "It has been an enjoyable but brief holiday from my homeland."

"Lebanon?"

"Egypt, Your Eminence. Alexandria is a rich land, and my home is open to you if ever you should visit, as your hospitality has been gracious toward me this night."

Everyone from North Korea to Belarus knew Muhammad ibn Affal was Egyptian, Corban understood, but he appreciated the caution of the *Sadhus*.

"When we heard there was someone interested in the American Christian, we were hesitant to respond to your inquiries, Cousin Muhammad."

"The Americans boast of their greatness, my *Sadhus*, but they only pollute our lands. It is a small matter to express my gratitude by adding to your great wealth—and allow my people to use this woman as a trophy against her own people, especially her father."

"You are brave to do this thing."

Corban nodded low again, but he knew the *Sadhus* would have used Kimberly Dench for his own trappings if the holy man's coffers had been more abundant, and his courage greater. This meeting had been made possible simply because Corban knew the Hindu man's riches were lacking.

"I do the work of the Holy One, and you work in your way. We each secure a spiritual reward, Your Eminence." Corban was ready for the transfer, but it would be impolite as a guest to bring up the subject of money. "A common enemy has made us friends."

"As you requested, she is unharmed." The *Sadhus* gestured to the figure in the center under the cloth. Even by candlelight, Corban could see she was listening, making small movements as they spoke. "We have our own methods here in India to punish Christians. But this is an occasion to make new bonds, even if it is with a Muslim."

"You are most gracious." Corban held up his hand to Kimberly. "May I?"

"Of course. She is to be yours after a small exchange."

Corban rolled onto his knees and lifted the front of Kimberly's veil. The candlelight illuminated a wide-eyed woman, not a girl at all. Her face was full of fear, punctuated by a dark bruise on her left cheek. A brown cord wrapped her wrists and attached to her neck.

"Very well." Corban returned to his cushion. "I will take her before the morning worshippers arrive."

"Then we have only one more item to arrange." The *Sadhus* produced a laptop from behind him and offered it to Corban. "I believe ten million Euros was the amount we agreed upon."

Placing the laptop on his lap, Corban repositioned his feet. In doing so, he stomped his heels hard on the carpeted floor, one after the other. It wasn't much of a signal, especially through the cement structure. But if Scanlon was listening with a hand on the support beam, he would understand the signal.

Taking his time, Corban logged into a bank on the Isle of Man, then transferred ten million Euros to the Indian account number at the top of the screen. He passed the laptop back to the *Sadhus* for confirmation.

Evidently, Scanlon had begun to disperse the lachrymator. Corban heard one of the gunmen cough and another sneeze on the walkway outside the tower.

"Perhaps she is worth more?" the *Sadhus* said, glancing at his gunmen, who seemed to follow every word, especially now. "What is five million more to you, the Great Muhammad?"

"Too small an amount, Your Eminence, to ruin our new friendship." Corban tensed, sensing the greed in the man's words. "There will be others in the future perhaps?"

"Of course." The *Sadhus* waved his hand, dismissing his previous words, but Corban wouldn't forget the man had been tempted to double-cross him. "You have a boat waiting. May you return to the Ganges as a pilgrim one day, Muhammad."

"Perhaps one day."

Corban stood as his eyes began to burn. The *Sadhus* coughed, obviously beginning to feel the effects of the gas as well. With an exaggerated gag, Corban doubled over and took a knee.

"What is this?" Corban pawed at the air as if he were choking. "Is it coming from the river?"

Before the *Sadhus* or his bodyguards could gather their wits for a response, Corban gripped Kimberly's arm and dragged her toward the door. He wasn't sure how much she could see through her heavy veil, but they needed to leave now. Kimberly was beginning to cough, and Corban's own eyes were watering, but the lachrymator was still safer than risking a double-cross by the *Sadhus* before Corban could make his getaway.

Outside, the chemical was denser, and Corban forced himself to remember he wasn't experiencing any permanent effects. Scanlon had warned him that tear gas was partially effective due to its victims not knowing what was traumatizing them.

The gunmen on the walkway were both blinded and breathless. Through his tears, Corban shoved Kimberly toward the front of the boat, threw off the bowline, and started the engine. He guessed he could've escaped the tower without Scanlon's help, but including him secured Kimberly's safety as well as implicated him in the safeguarding of Director Dench's daughter. And the operation tied Scanlon to Corban.

One mile upriver, Corban pulled up to a dock where Scanlon had recently arrived by motorcycle. The assassin smiled at them.

"Why again does your government want you dead?" Scanlon climbed into the boat as Corban was still wiping tears from his face. The Brit picked up Kimberly, who hadn't said a word, and hefted her onto the dock. With a knife, he carefully cut her binds and left her standing there. "I have generally appeased my conscience to some degree by killing, well, the bad guys. For your name to be given to me would usually confirm you were one of the worst."

Corban climbed from the boat and together they walked to the street where a car was parked. Scanlon welcomed Kimberly by holding the back door open for her, then he climbed into the driver's seat.

"You're sure you don't want to call her father?" Scanlon started the car.

"Not yet." Corban turned from the passenger's seat and shined a flashlight into Kimberly's face to gauge her well-being. Her eyes were alert though puffy, but she seemed fine otherwise. "What do you say, Kimberly? Mind if we take the scenic route home?"

"Not at all." She smiled. "Thank God for both of you."

CHAPTER NINE

The Protocol

Deputy Director William "Chip" Buchanen stood next to Director Jacob Dench in the parking lot on Boston's Boylston Street.

"It's like the old days, huh, Chip?" Dench puffed on a cigar, blowing smoke into the night sky. "Did you ever think we'd be standing here like this? We're minutes away from watching Corban Dowler beg us for his life."

"You don't know Corban very well, Jake." Chip eyed the tall buildings in the distance. "I still think we should've brought backup. There could be a sniper out there right now. The man we know as Scanlon doesn't normally take prisoners. Why's he bringing Corban to us alive?"

"It's a new age, Chip." Dench chuckled, but Chip

saw nothing laughable. "We should consider it an honor when an ally brings our enemy to us so we can personally eliminate him."

"I'm not killing Corban!"

"You signed off on Scanlon a week ago. Don't act like you've never gotten your hands wet!"

Chip cursed and walked over to his car, the door still open. He'd left it open intentionally in case he had to make a quick getaway. There were no free passes around Corban Dowler. Even if Dench had forgotten what it was like to be in the field, Chip remembered very well that in the spy world, nothing was guaranteed until a target was in the grave. But with Corban, even a body in the grave wasn't convincing enough.

"What're you doing?" Dench called from the front of his own car. "They'll be here any minute. You'll want to catch every minute of this."

"I'm reading a report from India about your daughter." Chip sat in the driver's seat, his tablet against the steering wheel, and scrolled through a daily activity report. "An agent in Varanasi filed a DAR on Kim. A Hindu extremist group led by someone called the *Sadhus* is the one who kidnapped her. But the word along the river is that he . . ."

"What, Chip? What'd they do to Kim?" Dench

stomped over to Chip's door. "We can catch a superspy, but we can't protect an American kid! What happened?"

"The Hindus sold her to an unknown Muslim, some big shot from Egypt. She's like a trophy to them, or maybe they mean to use her as leverage against you."

"Then they don't know me very well!" Dench scoffed. "The last three weeks my daughter's been missing, I've been focused on our security with Corban. They're crazy if they think I can be extorted to turn against my country, even if it is my daughter!"

"Yeah, you're all hugs and kisses, Jake. What do you want me to do about Kim?"

"There are a billion Muslims in the world. If one Muslim doesn't want to be found, he won't be. If he does, then we'll probably be the first to know. When Kim became a Christian and wanted to run around the world, she had to expect this sort of thing. Now she's got to live with her rotten choices and whatever they're doing to her!"

Chip was about to call him a cold-hearted father when a pair of headlights swung across them, and amplified sounds of the approaching vehicle caused a shiver to wash down Chip's body. As much as he'd meant to remain behind his car door for protection,

Chip moved to the front to see what was going to happen next. In that regard, Dench was right: he didn't want to miss this even if it killed him.

Dench stood five paces to Chip's right, in front of his car. Both vehicles' high beams illuminated the lot for three hundred yards directly ahead.

The approaching headlights belonged to an SUV, which stopped twenty paces in front of them. The headlights remained on, nearly blinding both men, but Chip focused on the dark windshield between the headlights. He imagined his old friend, Corban, watching him even then.

The driver's door opened and a sizeable black man stepped out. Chip recognized the middle-aged man, though he looked older than his outdated MI6 photo.

Chip waited as Scanlon walked slowly from his car door to the front of the SUV between the headlights. The man crossed his arms and stood there. Gazing around at the rest of the parking lot, all Chip could see was darkness. His ability to see beyond the lot was ruined by the bright lights. A whole army could be hiding out there . . . or no one at all.

"I've brought the man, Corban Dowler," Scanlon said, his deep voice filled with confidence and authority.

"That wasn't the deal." Dench lit another cigar. For a moment the flame from the lighter was close to his face and Chip saw the cut over the director's cheekbone. There were already whispers at the office speculating how he'd gotten the scar. Chip's money was on something sinister. "You were to kill the traitor. Where did you find him?"

"We'll get to that." Scanlon waited, unmoving. But why? Chip was becoming increasingly suspicious. Were there others in the SUV besides Corban? It seemed that Scanlon was stalling for some reason. "You should know that Corban Dowler saved my life during this operation."

"He what?"

"Twice. He saved my life twice."

"What do you mean he saved your life?" Dench shook his finger at Scanlon. "You're a professional! What Dowler did shouldn't matter to you. You were given a job to complete!"

"There's more." Scanlon said, uncrossing his arms. Chip glanced over his shoulder. If the shooting started, he hoped he could reach his car door in time. "Corban rescued . . . your daughter in India."

"Ha!" Dench guffawed and looked over at Chip. "You hear this nonsense?" He faced Scanlon again. "What game are you playing? We have intel that says otherwise—straight from operatives in India. Kim was sold to some Muslim from Egypt. She's not even in India anymore. And don't you worry about that Paris business. We've already made arrangements, Mr. Scanlon. Corban killed that agent in the airport."

"No, I killed the German agent," Scanlon said. "And Corban and I met with the German team in Frankfurt on our way here. Corban asked them to wait until after tonight to take me in, and they agreed. It was wrong for me to kill him, but they believe you are responsible for hiring too many operators for a single target. It was unprofessional. Crowding the field got a man killed. I have my own amends to make, but I'd say you're in more trouble than I am."

"Oh, no you don't! You don't strong-arm me, Scanlon!"

The passenger door of the SUV opened, and Corban stepped out. Chip's hand trembled. He wished he'd had a strong drink to take the edge off. Under his blazer, he felt his side arm, but something inside told him not to draw it, not to even move a muscle.

"Why isn't he in cuffs, Scanlon?" Dench yelled.

"Haven't you been listening?" Scanlon moved to his left to make room for Corban between the headlights of the SUV. "You're finished, Director."

"Finished?" Dench held up his cell phone. "One call, and one hundred agents will swarm this place. Tell me I'm finished again!"

"Your agents would never make it in time," Scanlon fired back. "You have no idea—"

Corban held up his hand, interrupting the assassin. Chip exhaled, relieved to find that Corban was truly in control, and not the MI6 operator. Dench didn't seem as certain of himself, however, as Corban walked briskly toward him.

"Chip, you should've been a better advisor here." Corban planted his feet three paces in front of Dench—close enough, Chip guessed, to reach Dench if he started to draw his weapon. "I'm disappointed in you, Chip. More than usual."

"Sorry, Corban. It got outta hand—you know, momentum of its own." Chip shook his head. "But you're right. No excuses. I messed up."

"Shut up, Chip!" Dench shouted. "We're the Agency! We're America! A traitor and a Brit don't tell us—"

"Director, you don't get to erase agents just because they become Christians." Corban's voice softened, but there was power in his words that made Chip's breathing difficult. "And you don't get to write off your daughter when she's persecuted in a distant land. Your heart has become so dark that you're not thinking clearly about the people who should mean the most to you."

"Corban Dowler, you can't take me down!" Dench drew a concealed handgun faster than anyone could stop him, and aimed it at Corban's face. "I have a kill order with your name on it. That doesn't go away! You're done!"

"You've just convinced me that I'm making the right move by leaving the Agency, even if you won't be there anymore." Corban hardly blinked at the sight of the gun. "You ruined yourself, Director. Chip, keep the next director a little better informed, huh?"

Raising his arm, Corban then dropped it like a race starter.

"I'm not done with you!" Dench screamed.

Kimberly Dench walked out from behind the SUV headlights. Chip recognized the oversized jean jacket she wore. It was one Corban sometimes wore around New York City when he wasn't on assignment. That meant Corban, Scanlon, and Kim had probably been in the country for a couple days, maybe even visiting Corban's home.

"Hi, Dad."

Dench stepped aside to keep Kim out of his line of fire.

"Kim, stay out of this! This changes nothing!" He pulled the hammer back on his handgun. "Remember who won tonight, Corban. Don't you forget it!"

"No, Jake, you remember tonight. And when you retire, you'll know that your actions brought you down. Your own sins have taken you over the edge."

Suddenly, other headlights beamed on around the parking lot, one after another, until the circle around them was complete and there was no more darkness. Chip guessed they'd driven up when the SUV had, the engine covering their approach. Or had they been there all along?

Chip heard two doors slam. He found that Corban and Scanlon had made their exits while he and Dench were distracted by the other lights. But distracted by whom?

There seemed only one answer.

The SUV backed away, its lights growing dimmer, then indistinguishable from the others.

Dench dropped his gun arm to his side as his daughter approached him.

"Who are they?" Dench gasped, turning in a circle.

"There's only one thing they can be." Chip took the gun from the director. "It's an Endgame

Protocol. He had a contingency plan all along, in case someone in the government turned against him. An agent like Corban Dowler can't just be erased. Think of all the lives he's saved over the years. Look what he did to Nace Scanlon! That man will never be the same. No, I'd say Corban belongs elsewhere. Let him go. He'll do greater things on his own. Look around you, Jake."

"I am looking around. What?" Dench seemed to shiver.

"I mean, *really look*. And think about it. How many Nace Scanlons are out there behind those lights?"

Shaking his head, Chip chuckled and took Kim by the arm.

"Drive you home, Miss Dench?"

CHAPTER TEN

The Beginning

Corban held the chair for Janice as she sat beside him in the busy steakhouse in Albany, New York. And like the spy he was, Corban had already surveyed the establishment for familiar faces and then requested a table with a view of the entire room.

"I hardly recognized you, sir," said Chloe Azmaveth, who sat with her husband, Zvi, across the table. "You know, without the fake nose and whatnot."

"Careful, Chloe, you'll ruin all the mystery for me," Janice said, then elbowed Corban in the arm. "We've been married for years, but I feel like I'm just getting to know him—or married to someone new."

"It's not a real marriage until Christ is your bond, anyway." Zvi, older and shorter than Chloe, saluted with his ice water. His Hebrew accent was rich and the friendliness on his face was genuine. "It was Christ who brought Chloe and me together."

"Well, I don't know if I'm ready for all this . . . secret agent stuff." Janice ducked her head as if she were dodging a drone flying above. "How do you do it, Chloe?"

The ex-Mossad agent smiled, and Corban appreciated her sense of discretion. He didn't need boastful agents working for him.

"There's a spiritual war waging," she said, narrowing her eyes at Corban, as if studying him. "It was a war declared long before us, but we're in the middle of it now. We can't sit in the bunker any longer."

"Chloe has told me a bit about your idea, Corban." Zvi leaned forward on the table. "You know, I'm a wealthy man. The gold business is thriving. Is that why we're here?"

Corban browsed the faces of the patrons again. He didn't recognize anyone nearby, but the government was sure to keep an eye on him for a while, maybe for the rest of his life.

Chip had arranged a deal for Corban's safe retirement, in exchange for his cooperation regarding the CIA assets he was still tied to after years with the Agency. Deal or not, Corban had lived too long near the dark edge to trust the Agency. Director Dench had resigned and Nace Scanlon had returned to Britain, but there would be new enemies, other assassins recruited from the darkness.

"Your financial support is welcome, Zvi, but this is about something bigger than money. I want to create a Christian intelligence and relief organization. It's time those of us with the skills and experience turn our trades into assets for believers in the field who need our support and protection."

"A Christian spy agency," Chloe said.

"Yes, but with more selflessness than your traditional spy agency." Corban took his wife's hand and held it firmly. Even though Janice had recovered from his faked dismissal of their marriage, he wondered if she was ready for the greater secrecy and subterfuge to come. "We'll hire Special Forces soldiers who are devout Christians, and deploy them with non-lethal weaponry to protect God's people in foreign nations. We'll smuggle Bibles, buy safe houses, and hide missionaries.

"As you two know, Chloe and I each have international networks already out there, and we'll need them. We'll pool our resources and start rescuing the persecuted, or at least we can make their calling more secure in some of the worst places on earth for Christians. I want tonight to be the beginning with the four of us. From here on, we live our lives a day at a time, ready to go be with our Lord, if necessary. But while we're here, we live it fully for God's people and the gospel message."

"Okay. I already left the IDF," Chloe said with a chuckle. "We're in. Just tell us what you want us to do, Corban."

"Janice is a nurse. I'd like her to coordinate our medical relief arm, which will sometimes be used as a cover."

"Yes, I can do that." Janice nodded. "I like the administration side of things."

"Zvi, you have business contacts world-wide. We don't need your money as much as we need your knowledge about moving equipment in and out of closed countries—your mining and assaying equipment. Your micron gold business will remain your cover as you go before us."

"You mean to smuggle Bibles hidden in my equipment?" Zvi tapped a finger on his chin. "Every country uses a different customs protocol. I'll get my people on the basics, then quietly format it for our own use."

"Good. Chloe, your cover will be as our public relations manager, but really, you'll be my second as our foreign operations manager. All rescue missions will pass your desk for approval, unless I'm not in the field. When I'm around, we'll work on field agent assignments together."

"So, I'm a handler?" Chloe sat back in her chair. "I like the sound of that. What will you do?"

"Well, I'll concentrate on security, as well as screening and hiring initial field agents. I'll also begin adjusting the minds of our foreign assets to demands we'll have for them. And where no one else can go, I can—like North Korea, Saudi Arabia, Iran, and Nigeria. My old aliases need to be maintained and covers need to remain intact. As you can guess, I'll be on the road a lot for security and rescue operations that'll be carried out by our teams."

"My nerves already feel like they're all . . . coiled up!" Janice said with a nervous chuckle. "What are we going to call ourselves?"

"I don't know." Corban said. "Some acronym that makes an impact."

"Janice just used the word *coil*," Chloe said. "I like the sound of that—a coil that springs into action. Can we use it as an acronym?"

"Hmm, coil. Okay. *C* for . . . Commission? You

know, like the Great Commission."

"How about International for the *I?*" Zvi asked.

"And *L* for Laborers," Janice said, "from Luke 10:2."

"That can be our theme verse! I know it in the King James Version," Chloe said. *"The harvest truly is great, but the laborers are few; pray ye, therefore the Lord of the harvest, that he would send forth laborers into his harvest.* So, what do you think, Corban?"

"*COIL,* the Commission of International Laborers, with theme verse of Luke 10:2. Great! That didn't take long. This is going to be some adventure . . ." Corban looked into their faces one at a time, knowing the testing that was probably ahead for them all. "There's only one thing left to do: let's pray . . . and never stop praying." Then Corban bowed his head.

~~~

BONUS CHAPTER ONE

Dark Liaison

Book One
The COIL Series

D.I. Telbat

BONUS CHAPTER ONE

Dark Liaison

Corban James Dowler had been shot before. This time was no different; the pain was no less. He stood in the shadow of a residential portico in Rome, Italy, gathering his senses before checking his wound. There was a dim streetlamp on the far corner but the light didn't reveal where he was hiding. The mass of moving water to his left was the Tiber River. Because of darkness, it was out of sight now, but he knew where he was. Of Rome's seven hills, the peak of Palatine was a stone's throw away. His rental car was ten blocks up the street to the north, but his destination was four blocks to the south.

Corban took stock of the wound in his left side. It felt like a million needles. Blood streamed down his leg, but it wasn't too serious. That love handle would never be the same, but he was thankful that the bullet had missed his kidney and ribs.

He eased farther back into the shadows as a lean man crept into the street and then paused. The man still held the silenced pistol that he'd used to shoot Corban. There was only one reason the assassin was standing in the street: he wanted to finish Corban off. The man waited, listening, twenty yards away.

Corban took off his glasses. His eyes were fine. The glasses were part of his costume. He blamed his current wound on his costume. Tonight he was Muhammad ibn Affal, an alias from his past that opened more doors in the Middle East than anywhere, but resulted in misfortune in places like Rome. It was his most accessible alias, requiring little prep-time; he'd had little choice but to use it on this emergency visit to Italy.

His foe still stood in the street, listening to the night. The slightest whisper of clothing would alert this predator. Nevertheless, Corban was calm as he disassembled his eyewear. Pulling off both earpieces, he was left with two stubby, straight lengths still connected to the frame. No one ever noticed that the frame itself was unusually thick and round as a pencil.

The man in the street seemed to look right at him, but Corban knew the darkness hid him. Corban also knew his foe was debating if he should venture into that darkness to investigate.

The assassin slinked toward the portico's shadow, his pistol leveled and sweeping.

Pressing both frame lengths toward the lenses, Corban aimed each end at his foe. Since he knew the armed delay of his miniature weapon, he counted the seconds. It was calibrated for ten yards, but this was a little close to use on a man with a drawn pistol.

A tiny red laser beam shot out. When Corban saw the red dot on the man's chest, he instantly crouched low against the building in anticipation. The sharp pop of a CO_2 cartridge sent a tranquilizer dart tipped with falaco into the man's chest, right where Corban's laser sight had beamed. In return, two silenced rounds from the pistol slammed into the wall over Corban's head and peppered him with white dust. Like ricin, falaco required two beats of the heart to reach the vital organs. It was a powerful narcotic that would have killed the man if had the dart been dipped in more than a tiny drop of the toxin upon preparation.

The killer shuddered on his feet, then crumbled in place on the edge of the street.

Reassembling his glasses, Corban put them back on his face. If his foe wasn't alone, Corban would be in trouble. Though he had other non-lethal weapons at headquarters in New York City, he'd brought only the glasses on this trip.

Corban smoothed down his fake beard and mustache, both trimmed and styled in the most loyal Islamic fashion. Ignoring his trickling wound, he stepped out of the shadows and into the quiet street. Kneeling next to the killer, he checked the man's weapon: a 9-millimeter, custom-made, machine pistol with a French label. Corban had never seen one like it, which meant the man was a professional, a hunter-tracer of some type.

Rolling the man over, he dragged him out of the street. Falaco's effects would last for an hour, but no more. Though Corban was in a hurry, he was curious, as well. He checked the man's pockets. Two packs of chewing gum and a pack of cigarettes, but no matches or lighter. Corban was tempted to keep the cigarettes, but he decided against it. One never knew what the new generation of spies and assassins carried. It could be a transponder or even a bomb that would explode two steps away from its recognized body heat signature.

Studying the assassin's face up close, Corban engraved his features into his mind. The man was not over forty. His face was lean, cold, and clean-shaven, and he had black hair and bushy eyebrows. He appeared to be Italian. The Italian government was not hunting Muhammad ibn Affal, but he was on more than a few countries' watchdog lists. To them, he was an arms thief and smuggler—a terrorist. Such an alias was generally safe to use, even near Western countries that knew him well. But they were only supposed to watch him, not kill him. If someone wanted his identity gone, something in the world of terror had shifted.

Finished with his examination, Corban left the killer and jogged across the street. He slowed to a walk and entered a vine-crowded alley. Pausing every twenty paces, he listened to the night: the city traffic in the distance, a dog yelping, but no trailing footsteps.

A few blocks later, Corban put his back to a telephone pole and watched his target house and the surrounding neighborhood for several minutes. The Italian assassin, even if he woke early, would not know Corban was coming here. Or would he? Every stage was a potential ambush. The Italian could have followed him from the airport, or perhaps he began to tail him later. If his rental car was marked with a transponder, it didn't matter. He wasn't going back for it.

Corban kept a watchful eye on the house. It had a short, stone wall around its front courtyard. An ornate fountain sat dry and littered, molding from whatever last rains had graced its bowl. An old Audi was parked in the driveway. There were no lights on in the house. He knew it was a four-bedroom residence with a pool in the rear. The whole place reeked of neglect, but Corban expected no less. With the death threats that Tye and Sarah Mentolla had been receiving from extremists, he didn't blame them for remaining in the safety of their home and calling for help.

It was an age-old struggle that had started in the 1500s—apostate teaching versus the biblical teaching that came out of the Protestant Reformation. The Mentollas had been Christian missionaries in Rome for nine years, trained to reach apostates specifically. But the superstitions of the people had won over the washing of Christ's redemptive blood this day.

The Mentollas' dog had been killed a week ago, and the phone calls were becoming more threatening by the day. Just sixteen hours ago, their house had been stoned. Normally, other field agents would have handled this volatile situation, but they were in demand elsewhere. It was up to Corban to get them out this time.

He saw headlights far up the street. Climbing over the Mentollas' stone wall, Corban pushed through the bushes that choked a brick walkway until he reached the back door of the house. As suspected, the backyard pool was filthy, but drained. He was about to knock on the door when he heard breaking glass and shouts from the street. Jogging back to the walkway, he saw a car stopped in front of the house. A half dozen youths were throwing rocks at the windows as another lit a Molotov cocktail.

Returning to the back door, Corban kicked it in. Wood splintered around him as he barged through the frame into the house. From there, he could see through the dining and living rooms to the front window. As he watched, the cocktail crashed through broken glass. Flames engulfed the carpet.

A child cried, and Corban heard voices from down the hallway to his right. The thugs in front were lucky Corban was not the man he once was—a man who went heavily armed on every mission. He would've had no qualms about dashing into the street with his Beretta and . . .

But Corban was no longer that man. God had changed him six years before. Since then, he could not bring himself to kill. He had to retire from the CIA early, his pension only a few years away, yet his convictions intact. In many ways, though, he was still that old spy tracker. Even though he was fifty-six and not in the best physical condition, he still felt like a man of twenty. After years of honing his skills, he could move like a panther and think like a computer. He was the last of the old-school spies, and although he no longer used his craft for the government, he still used it—to preserve the defenseless.

Fire reflected off his forehead and glasses as he stared at the growing flames. A man shouted at him in Italian. Corban recognized Tye Mentolla right away. He'd never met his family, but Corban knew them well. The man was carrying his four-year-old daughter, Lacy. Six-year-old Forest was behind his father, clinging to his panic-stricken mother, Sarah. Corban couldn't speak much Italian, but he didn't need to—the Mentollas were Americans.

"I'm here to help you," Corban said over the roar of the fire. The father didn't move. "Sixteen hours ago, you called your mission board in the States, requesting emergency leave. I'm here to get you out. Carry what you can. The fire's still low, but we don't have much time. Quick! We'll leave out the back."

"They told me no one would be here for another week," Tye said, shaking his head. "The threat level wasn't high enough, they said."

"Fine. You want to stay here?"

Coughing at the smoking flames, Tye set his daughter down on the floor.

"Quick!" he urged his family. "Go get dressed!"

His children scampered down the hallway.

"I'll get the albums." Sarah hurried to a display cabinet against a wall. A stone thrown from outside bounced off the floor and hit her leg. She screamed and dropped a handful of photos. "Tye, help me!"

"Sarah, go get your clothes and help the kids!" Tye said as he knelt to gather the pictures from the floor. He muttered a prayer for safety and kept a wary eye on the encroaching flames. "I never thought it would come to this. After all our work."

Corban spotted movement from the corner of his eye. He pivoted to face a tall form in a hooded sweatshirt looming in the back doorway. It was one of the thugs he'd seen in the street. The chiseled shape of a machete rose to strike down at Corban. Shifting his feet, Corban heel-kicked the youth in the solar plexus, sending him skidding across the patio and into the empty pool. Corban heard the thug gasping for air and knew the hooded figure would be fine once he caught his breath.

". . . and so that's when I called the board," Tye was saying. He turned to Corban, oblivious of Corban's confrontation with the youth. "What'd you say your name was?"

"I didn't say."

"Oh."

"Maybe you should get dressed, too, Mr. Mentolla."

Tye nodded and jogged down the hallway. Corban spied the growing flames while keeping an eye on the back door. Sarah soon emerged, pinning her hair up and helping Lacy into a sweatshirt, then Tye and Forest came from the hallway together, both carrying their Bibles. Sarah picked up her purse and a small bag.

"Do you have a plan?" Tye asked, gathering the stack of folders and albums. "We'll never get our car out with them blocking the way."

These were good, caring people, Corban thought as he watched Forest tug a baseball cap down over his brow. He hated to see the darkness overwhelm the light so horribly.

He turned toward the pool and the semi-darkness.

"Follow me."

~~~

For more information about *Dark Liaison*, visit our book page at ditelbat.com/book/dark-liaison/. To see all books in *The COIL Series*, visit ditelbat.com/coil-series/.

~

Please leave your comments wherever you bought or downloaded this book. Reviews tremendously help authors, and David Telbat takes reader input into consideration when making his future publishing plans. Thanks for reading!

ABOUT THE AUTHOR

D.I. Telbat desires to honor the Lord with his life and writing. Many of his stories focus on persecuted Christians worldwide—their sacrifice, their suffering, and their rescues.

David studied writing in school and worked for a time in the newspaper field, but he is now doing what he loves most: writing and Christian ministry. At this time, he lives in California, but keeps his home base in the NW US. See his complete bio at ditelbat.com/about/.

His Telbat's Tablet website at ditelbat.com offers FREE weekly Christian short stories, or related posts, which include his novel news, author reflections, and occasional challenges for today's Christian. Subscribe to his weekly blog at ditelbat.com to have his posts delivered right to your inbox, plus receive exclusive subscriber gifts!

Made in the USA
Lexington, KY
15 July 2019